This Ladybird

This Ladybird retelling
by
Molly Perham

Published by Ladybird Books Ltd
80 Strand London WC2R 0RL
A Penguin Company
20
© LADYBIRD BOOKS LTD 1993

Printed in Italy

FAVOURITE TALES

The Town Mouse and the Country Mouse

illustrated
by
KEN McKIE

based on an Æsop fable

Country Mouse lived in a small house deep in the roots of an old tree. One day his cousin Town Mouse came to visit him.

"Welcome to my home," said Country Mouse. "You will love the country. It is so nice and quiet."

Country Mouse made a big supper and they sat down to eat at the wooden table. But Town Mouse did not like the plain food, or the thick mugs and plates.

And the little straw bed made Town
Mouse scratch and sneeze.

"It's too dark and quiet in the
country," he said.
"I can't sleep."

Every morning before the sun was up, Country Mouse was busy finding food to store up for the winter.

"Come and help me, Cousin," he shouted cheerfully.

But Town Mouse did not want to work. He did not like getting his hands and clothes dirty.

"In town there is no need to look for food," he grumbled.

One day Country Mouse took Town Mouse across the meadow to find some mushrooms.

The horse who lived there came to make friends with the mice. Town Mouse was so surprised he fell head over heels in the wet grass.

"I don't like the country," he said. "It's cold, it's wet, and it's very frightening!"

On the way home Town Mouse was so busy telling Country Mouse about the town that he did not notice a huge owl swooping down towards him.

"Look out!" shouted Country Mouse, pushing his cousin into a ditch. The owl flew away. But what a fright they'd both had!

Town Mouse hated the country more
than ever. It was cold, and wet, and
frightening – and very dangerous! He
wanted to go home.

Later that night Town Mouse saw a
family who lived at the end of the lane
getting into their car to go to town.

"Come on, Cousin," he cried.
"You can see the town
for yourself. Let's go!"

The two mice hid under the back seat
of the car until they reached the
middle of the town. Then they
jumped out into the busy street.

Horns hooted and cars whizzed past. Country Mouse had never heard so much noise or seen so many bright lights.

Town Mouse took his cousin home
with him. But the house was much too
big for poor Country Mouse.

"I'm sure to get lost,"
he thought nervously.

The town mice prepared a huge feast of fruit, cakes, puddings and cream. It was all too rich and sweet for Country Mouse, and he began to feel sick.

Next day Country Mouse found a nice piece of cheese. He didn't realise that it was a trap!

Town Mouse and his family rescued poor Country Mouse just in time. But they were all seen by the cat and had to run for their lives back to their hole in the wall.

Country Mouse was so afraid now that he hardly dared to move around.

At bedtime Country Mouse did not like his soft little bed. And the room was too bright because of the lights in the street.

When at last he fell asleep, Country Mouse dreamed of home.

He could smell the trees and the fresh earth. Oh, how he wished he was safely back in his country home once more – especially as it would soon be Christmas.

In the morning the mice found a large hamper under the Christmas tree.

Town Mouse read the label. "It's going near your home!" he cried to his cousin.

Country Mouse jumped right into the hamper. Soon it was carried outside and put into a van.

That afternoon Country Mouse tumbled out of the van into the lane where he lived. He could hear carol singing coming from the church and went closer to listen.

He sighed with happiness.

It had been a great adventure, but now all he wanted was to forget it and enjoy Christmas. He was safely home at last!